www.harpercollinschildrens.com

ISBN 978-0-06-274855-3

18 19 20 21 22 PC 10 9 8 7 6 5 4 3 2 1 ❖ First Edition

Designed by Brenda E. Angelilli and Scott Petrower

My Fanciest Things

Written by
Krista Tucker

Illustrated by
Grace Lee

HARPER
An Imprint of HarperCollins*Publishers*

For Gaiee, who taught me that simple
can also be extraordinary.
And to Nancy Kanter—whose passion and dedication
to Nancy Clancy has given so many of us
the chance to fill our hearts with fancy!
—Krista

For my husband, Emery, who fills my life
with the fanciest thing of all.
—Grace

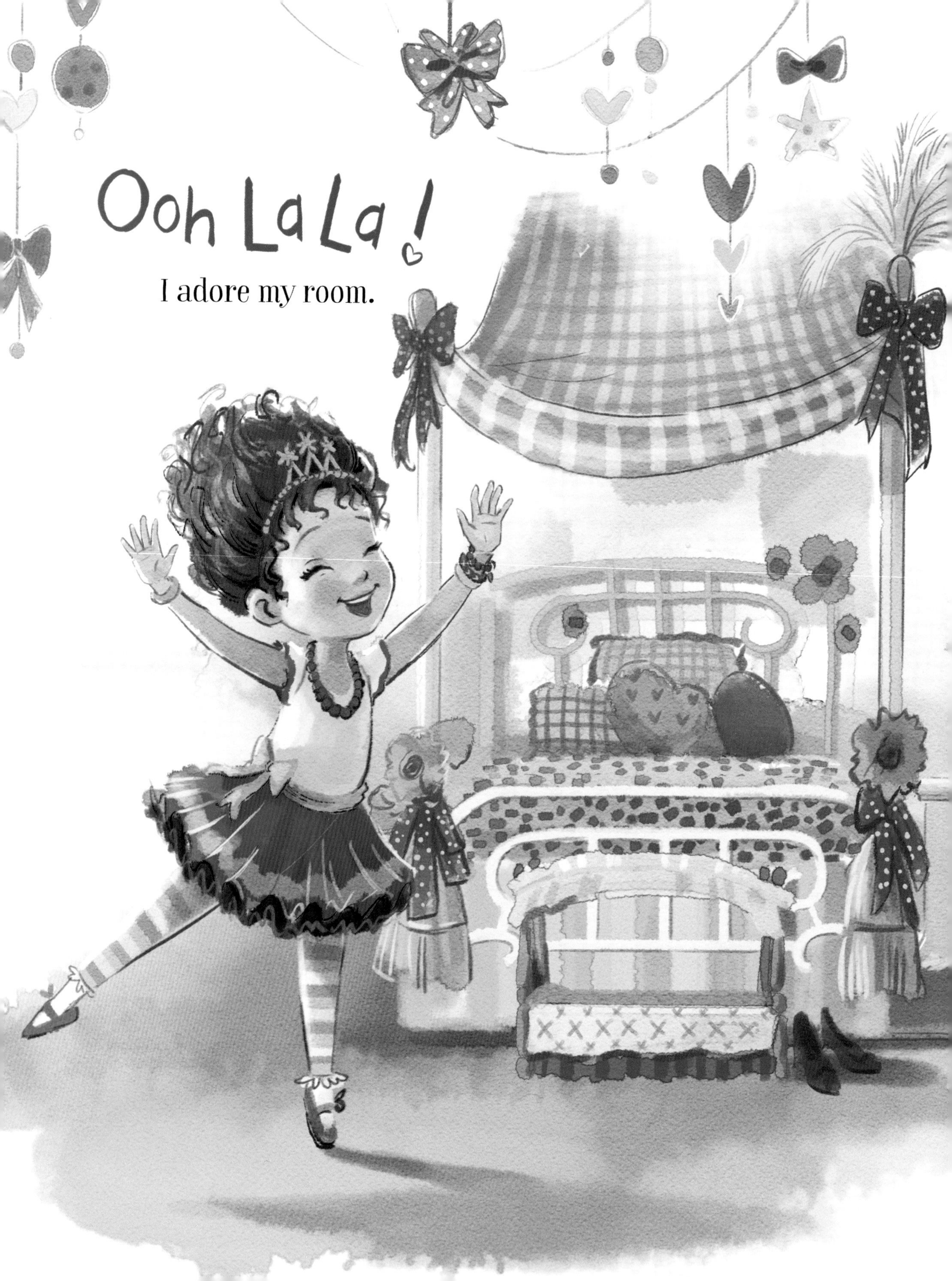

I adore my room.

It's filled with all
my favorite **fancy** things.

I love butterflies, so my best friend, Bree, and I made these wings.

Aren't they Sublime?

That's a fancy word for beautiful.

We spend hours and hours in the backyard, fluttering around like **papillons.**

That's French for butterflies.

It is one of my favorite things we do together!

This fabulous tutu is from my dance recital.

Our dance teacher, Madame Lucille, said our performance was stupendous!

That's fancy for really good! I will always remember how wonderful Bree and I felt when everyone applauded at the end.

Mom gave me this tea set. It's so exquisite! That's a fancy word for lovely.

I'm almost one hundred percent positive it is why my tea always tastes so delicious.

It makes tea for two with Bree parfait.

That's French for perfect.

Sometimes we let my little sister, JoJo, join us.

Voilà!
Tea for three.

JoJo was so sweet to give me this picture she drew of us.
Not to brag, but I'm practically an expert at being a big sister.

I put JoJo's drawing in this frame and decorated it with glitter and jewels so it sparkles like my tiara. Whenever JoJo sees it, she smiles.

Once when I had a cold that was worse than awful, Mom made me this pillow with real lace! I'm certain that one day it will become a family heirloom,

which is fancy for old and special.

My boas make everything fancier!

Let me demonstrate.
(That's fancy for show you.)
Here's ordinary Frenchy . . .

Ta-da!

Frenchy becomes
extraordinary!

Sometimes Dad will even be silly and wear one of my boas when we play dress up.

This gorgeous vanity used to belong to my grandma. It is one of Grandpa's most treasured possessions, because it reminds him of her.

But Grandpa gave it to me because he knew I would love it as much as Grandma did.

When I think about it, each one of my fancy things reminds me of somebody I love!

And you know what?

Love
might just be the
fanciest
thing of all!